For Mum, Dad
Rachel and Ben.

ISBN 978-0-244-67122-8

DADDY'S BRILLIANT BEARD

Katherine Turner

I love my Daddy's enormous beard.

Daddy loves his beard too;
he thinks it's very useful...

It's also starting to smell
a little Strange . . .

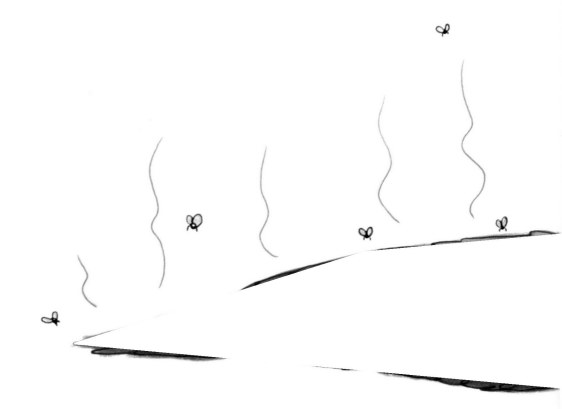

Daddy and I decided to go for a bike ride to freshen up his stinky beard!

We pedalled up the tallest hill . . .

BARBERS
THIS WAY

"Perhaps it's time to say goodbye to my beard, sighed Daddy.

But on the way to the barbers, we heard an alarm coming from the local bakery!

"Come back!! STOP!"
shouted Mrs Crumpet.

Two sneaky thieves had pinched
Mrs Crumpet's special cakes...

...and were making a run for it!

"Leave it to me," said Daddy.
"I have a plan!"

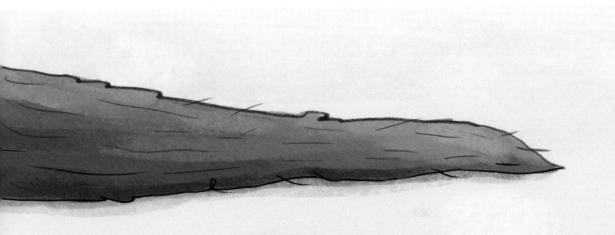

Daddy 'swirled' his beard up in a giant lasso and circled it wildly over his head!

Daddy's beard **whipped** round
the ankle of the first thief,

causing them both to **tumble** to the ground like *skittles...*

...as cakes **sprung** from their hands!

The cakes landed perfectly on Daddy's **stretched-out** beard.

"We've been after these two for weeks!" said PC Fred.

Daddy Still gets himself into lots of trouble...

...but no one can live without his BRILLIANT beard!

The
END

Katherine studied fine art at Canterbury Christ Church University and graduated in 2009. Since then she has been working as a freelance painter and illustrator.

Her illustrations are created through a combination of watercolour and digital media.

'Daddy's Brilliant Beard' is her first picture book.

www.ktdesigns.me